Gateway to the West

SUSETTE WILLIAMS

Hope for the Heart

THANKSGIVING BOOKS & BLESSINGS

Book 1: GONE TO TEXAS
By Caryl McAdoo
Book 2: GATEWAY TO THE WEST
By Susette Williams
Book 3: TRAIL TO CLEAR CREEK
By Kit Morgan
Book 4: HEART AND HOME
By P. Creeden
Book 5: NO TURNING BACK
By Lynette Sowell
Book 6: DAUGHTER OF DEFIANCE
By Heather Blanton
Book 7: NUGGET NATE: MOYA'S THANKSGIVING PROPOSAL
By George McVey
Book 8: UNMISTAKABLY YOURS
By Kristin Holt
Book 9: ESTHER'S TEMPTATION
By Lena Nelson Dooley

Dedication

I can never thank my family enough for the encouragement and support they give me and each other. Thank you all for dealing with my deadlines and weird writing schedule. I love and appreciate all of you!

Thank you, to my readers. It blesses my heart to know you connect with my stories and characters. I also appreciate the kind reviews and the time you spend with me, delving into my stories. Thank you for sharing a part of your day with me. I hope that I have been able to make you smile or brightened your day in some way. Thank you for your continued support.

Acknowledgement

I hope you will enjoy this story, along with the other books in the THANKSGIVING BOOKS & BLESSINGS series. I can't thank you enough for your continued support and hope that you are truly blessed in the year to come—Thank You!

Gateway to the West

Book 2

1840

SUSETTE WILLIAMS

Hope for the Heart

This book is a work of fiction. Any references to historical events, real people, or real places are used fictitiously. Other names, places, characters, and events are products of the author's imaginations, and any resemblance to actual events or places or persons, living or dead, is entirely coincidental.

© 2018 by **Susette Williams**

First Edition September 7, 2018

Printed and bound in the United States of America

ISBN: 9781720136422
AISN (eBook): **B07FP79G6M**

Chapter One

Bear ye one another's burdens, and so fulfil the law of Christ.
Galatians 6:2

Independence, Missouri — June 1, 1840

*H*āley *Hunter's jutted jaw and cute* upturned nose exuded a sense of confidence and determination. Yet the pleading looks in her eyes hinted at an underlying vulnerability. She planted her fists firmly on her hips, her reticule dangling from the drawstrings clasped within her grip. "Well, do you or don't you need a cook?"

"I do." Malcom Wheeler recalled saying those words a long time ago, and he hadn't been there, not when she needed him. It was a mistake he would never make again.

"Then it's set." Haley smiled.

"Wait, no." Malcom shook his head vehemently. "You can't do that. I wasn't finished speaking."

"Well, it appears you are now." She picked up a green floral valise, clasping it firmly in her hands. "Show me the way."

Malcom gritted his teeth. The cook he originally hired for

the job had backed out. He wanted to find another man for the job. Heck, he was willing to do it himself if he had the time and forethought to planning meals. His job was to lead the wagon train and get everyone to their destination in one piece, with their scalps intact.

"It ain't safe for a woman." His jaw clenched. He could be as stubborn and unmoving as she was—even more.

Her eyebrow arched. "Then why are you taking women with you on the wagon train?"

"Because they're married." And from what he could tell, she wasn't. She'd be a distraction to several of the other single men, and he needed everyone to have their wits about them.

"I am… I was…" Her mouth clamped shut, giving him a moment of peace and satisfaction. It only seemed to fuel her determination. "So, if something happens to one of the men during the trip, you just toss their wife by the wayside?" Haley asked. "Perhaps leave them for the Indians?"

"No." Haley infuriated him more than fur flying in a cat fight. "It's my job to protect the members of my wagon train, and I take my job very seriously."

"Perhaps you think it best if I tried to make it on my own, without the protection of a larger group?" Her attempt at pious indignation wrenched his gut.

"Why is it so important to you that you insist on going?"

"I have to find my brother and his family." Haley wiped her left eye. "Now that I am a widow and alone in a strange land, I need to go be with what family I have left here."

Crying didn't work on him, or at least not any more. But he was concerned about her safety. A woman alone could be in just as much danger in a town like this as she would be on the trail. "What about your parents?"

"They are in Britain." Her voice quivered. "We said our goodbyes when we came to this country, knowing full well we might not see them again. My brother and I had hoped to make our way here with our families and then send for our parents."

Malcom wasn't happy. Not one bit. He grunted in frustration, knowing full well everyone from the wagon train was lined up and ready to leave. His every move was on display. While the cook he had lined up to cook for his crew and some of the single men had backed out, he questioned his own sanity at allowing a woman with no family to join the wagon train. Tiny Tim, who wasn't the least bit tiny, had a habit of burning food on the campfire. One would think a man that size could cook. His talents apparently lay more in consuming vittles than preparing them. What choice did Malcom really have? And that infuriated him even more. "Come with me."

He led Haley to the Van Der Heims' wagon and introduced her to the middle-aged couple, Martha and Jonathan. "I don't know if the two of you would mind allowing Miss Hunter to ride with you in your wagon. It would be greatly appreciated."

"We would be happy to have you, Miss Hunter." Martha's eyes brightened. "Jonathan is the love of my life, but not the talkative type."

"Not that you give me a chance to get a word in edgewise." Jonathan gave his wife a sideways glance and winked. "Now I'll have two chatterboxes to keep me company on the long journey."

"Does this mean I am hired?" Haley looked at him with questioning eyes. "If so, I have my own wagon." She flashed an apologetic glance at the Van Der Heims.

Nick took his hat off and ran his hand through his hair before replacing it. He wanted to shout or throw his hands and his hat up in the air in frustration. "Pray tell, who is going to drive this wagon for you?"

He knew the answer before she even spoke. That defiant chin raised. "I'm quite capable."

"Of course, you are." His tone was sarcastic, not meant to encourage her, but none-the-less, she smiled. "Bring your wagon up alongside the Van Der Heims' and then when we pull out in ten minutes you can pull in front of them." Malcom focused his attention on Jonathan. "I hope you won't mind keeping an eye on Miss Hunter? It would certainly put my mind to rest."

Malcom caught a glimpse of Haley still standing there. "Yes?"

"I'm sorry." She laughed nervously. "It will take me a little time to get my wagon hitched. Do you think you could send someone to help me?"

He stood there, dropped jaw, staring at her. "Are you serious?"

She nodded like an innocent deer, unaware it was about to become another animal's prey.

Grabbing Haley's arm firmly at her elbow, he excused himself and lead her toward the back of the wagon before realizing he had no idea where her wagon even was.

He noticed Colby Jackson riding in their direction. Colby had a habit of making his acquaintance with everyone before they left on the trail. Malcom knew he did it so that he could scout out the most eligible fillies in the group, not that the young buck was ready to settle down.

"Colby." Malcom motioned for him to head their way.

It didn't take two seconds for Colby's gaze to dart toward Malcom's companion. Haley was a beautiful woman and he knew he'd be protecting her honor as well as her life bringing her on this journey. Instead of having Colby help Haley get her horse and wagon hitched, he'd do it himself.

Colby brought his horse to a stop five feet in front of them. He tipped his hat at Haley. "Howdy, ma'am."

She smiled and greeted him in turn.

"Since you're already making your rounds," Malcom's tone was curt, "I need you to make sure everyone has everything they need before we leave. I have to help Miss Hunter get her wagon hitched so we can get on the trail."

"Yes, sir." Colby winked and tipped his hat again to Haley. "Pleasure meeting you, Miss Hunter."

"Likewise." While polite, Haley didn't appear the least bit starry-eyed over Colby. Which undoubtedly took the young stud's ego down a notch. All the girls swooned over him like he was the last piece of dessert and they couldn't wait to devour him. It was refreshing to see a woman who didn't fall for his charm.

"Come along." Malcom loosened his grip on her elbow but held it firm enough to still urge her to continue moving. "Where did you say your wagon and horses were?"

"The stable."

He nodded and headed there with her in tow.

"You're going to learn to do this yourself," Malcom said. "I can't guarantee there will always be someone available to help you and you need to be able to pull your own weight on the trail."

"I'm a quick learner," Haley said. "Just teach me what to do."

Malcom showed her how to put on the horse's harness and had her do the other one. Then he led one of the horses in front of the wagon while she repeated his steps with the second horse. He taught her how to back it up and connect the center shaft to the pole strap of their harness. Then he collected the reins and tossed them onto the driver's seat of the wagon.

"Let me help you in the wagon."

"Thank you." Haley retrieved her reticule and valise from where she'd laid them on the ground while they worked. She placed the valise on the floorboard of the wagon and set her reticule on the seat.

He placed a hand on either side of her waist. His face warmed as his chest constricted. Sara was the last woman he'd ever touched so intimately. Memories of her touch, or the feel of her lips against his had been fading. Haley reignited the sensation he'd once felt.

Malcom didn't deserve happiness. He shouldn't even be alive. He should have died protecting his family—but he didn't. He wasn't even there to look out for them when they needed him most. His throat went dry. He tried to swallow in order to moisten his mouth. Looking out for Haley would be a form of penance to make up for his past.

Without a second thought, he hopped up into the wagon beside Haley.

Chapter Two

*H*aley *brushed strands of hair off of* her face as beads of perspiration trickled down her temple. Missouri was hot in June, and from what she understood, this was only a precursor to what lay ahead. Thankfully, Malcom had informed her they would be stopping shortly, and to follow the other wagons to form a circle.

She knew very little about the man, other than the fact that he was both rugged and handsome. His features were stern. He was undoubtedly a strong man both physically and emotionally. Haley prayed for him and their journey. He was obviously under pressure, undertaking the task of leading twenty-seven wagons across many terrains. In her anxiousness to find a way to travel with others to find her brother and his family, she hadn't asked how long the journey would take. She'd purchased many provisions which had drained what money she'd had left.

"Why did you have to go and leave me, Thomas?" Haley knew it wasn't her husband's choice. The good Lord took whom He chose, and it was apparently Thomas' time to go. She often wondered if it was sickness that weakened him, or if his will to continue had given up when eight years of marriage had produced no children. Hope had turned to despair, discouragement and even a touch of bitterness, which he'd tried to hide. But she knew he felt it—not towards her, but towards God. The doctor said he didn't see any reason for her inability to produce a child, yet her womb had remained barren. Was Malcom married? Did he have children? She had seen a couple wagons that had children on them. Maybe one of them belonged to him. It would be nice to befriend a couple with children. Haley missed her niece and nephew. They were her only chance to interact with children, other than helping new mothers out at church.

She'd had to become content with what she had, often reminding herself of the scripture, *'I know both how to be based, and I know how to abound: every where and in all things I am instructed both to be full and to be hungry, both to abound and to suffer need.'* She did not need a child, but she'd wanted one. So, had Thomas. Blaming God or each other would not make the pain or the longing go away, so she'd chosen to focus on the blessings she did have, and even those were dwindling as the days ticked on, like an hourglass running out of time.

A gentle breeze gave her a moment of refreshment. Haley watched and followed as the wagons in front of her began to detour as they wrapped around into a circle, coming to a halt. Nervous energy coursed through her as her mind flooded with a gazillion questions. It occurred to her that she hadn't asked how many people she would be preparing food for, or if she would have anyone to assist her in her endeavors.

Haley climbed down from her wagon and absorbed her surroundings. This looked like a spot that had been utilized before. Perhaps it was a regular stopping place for wagon trains. There was a spot cleared in the center that had ashes long ago extinguished, with traces of burnt wood not totally consumed by the fires. She noticed bushes a short walking distance from the site. It would be a wonderful treat if there were wild blueberries that she could use to make a dessert for dinner, or perhaps use in flapjacks the next morning for breakfast.

"Rest up while you can." Malcom startled her. She turned toward him.

"I asked Eli to come water your horses for you." Even though he was being considerate, Malcom showed about as much emotion as a totem pole as he spoke with her, but his eyes said more than his facial expressions had to offer. "I'll take you over to the chuck wagon and go over things with you, so you at least know what you're dealing with when we stop for dinner. I won't have time to get you situated then, so you'll have to make do."

"Thank you." Haley followed alongside Malcom, asking him questions about who she would be cooking for and if she would have any help.

"There are four other hired hands besides me. You've already met Colby, and Galen Marshfield will also be joining us for meals. Unless of course he decides to join any of the other wagons for occasional meals."

Haley had never been on a wagon train before. Relief flooded her, knowing she wouldn't have to cook for the entire camp. "Will any of the men be helping to build the fire to cook on?"

His lips formed a rigid line. "For you, I'll make an exception."

"Thank you." She tilted her head, giving a small nod of appreciation. The less she said, the better. While her husband never minded her spirited conversation, she knew few men revered outspoken women. Haley couldn't help but wonder if there was a reason he was so abrasive towards her. He obviously struggled to keep his tongue in check as much as she did.

"I should warn you that the trail gets lonely." Malcom peered intently into her eyes. "Be careful not to put yourself in compromising situations with any of the men folk."

Until a couple months ago, Haley had a husband to look out for her, so it wasn't a concern. She struggled to think of herself the way others perceived her if they didn't know. Malcom knew though, she'd told him earlier, before he'd hired her and now he was being kind enough to look out for her needs. "Thank you. I appreciate your concern."

After Malcom finished going over the expectations with her and he went on to tend to his tasks, she retrieved a couple buckets. Thankfully, she would only be obligated to prepare breakfast and supper but would need to prepare some extra biscuits for the men to eat during the day on the trail. While she had a little time now, she made use of one of the cows Malcom had brought on the trail for fresh milk. She hung the bucket beneath her wagon. Fresh butter would be wonderful for supper. Perhaps she'd mix in some cinnamon and honey for extra flavor. Once she completed that task, she went in search of berries.

The bushes she spotted when they came to this campsite did have blueberries and some of them were ripe. Haley knelt down to pick them from the vine.

"What are you doing?"

Haley startled. She stood up to greet the plain-looking young woman standing next to her. The girl appeared to be maybe fifteen or sixteen. Her bonnet covered blonde hair pulled back into a bun. A pale blue floral dress seemed a bit fancy for the trail, especially since it looked new.

"I'm picking blueberries for dessert tonight." Haley smiled warmly at the girl. "My name is Haley. What's yours?"

"I'm Macey." She curtseyed. "Do you mind if I ask you something?"

"No, what would you like to know?"

"You don't appear to have a fella." Macey twisted about, casting a glance toward camp and then back at Haley. "I wondered what your feelings toward Colby were?"

She couldn't help but laugh. "I'm sorry." It took a moment to compose herself. Haley realized that to a girl like Macey, this was very serious. The girl was obviously infatuated with him. "I can assure you I have no feelings for the young man." Haley's expression sobered. "Truth be told, I'm recently widowed and not looking for a new husband."

"I'm glad." Macey's cheeks flushed. "I'm sorry. That didn't

come out right."

"How long have you had a crush on him?" Haley grinned. She remembered what it was like to fall in love.

"Since last year when he almost ran me over coming out of the mercantile." Macey's eyes brightened. Her face quickly turned to panic. "Promise me you won't tell him?"

Making an X across her heart, Haley said, "I promise."

Macey's eyes widened. She pointed, opening her mouth to scream, but nothing came out.

Haley turned in time to see the snake maybe six feet from where they stood. She wrapped her arm around Macey and started dragging her backwards.

A shot rang out. Then another, splattering the snake.

Her heart raced even faster as she saw Malcom close the distance between them in long strides.

"What in the world were you thinking?" Malcom glared at her with green, steely eyes. "Never wander off without telling me."

"I'm not that far from the wagons," Haley protested. "You could clearly see me." She felt like a child being reprimanded.

"Grab your things and get back to the wagon." His jaw tensed. "We need to get back on the trail." He turned to walk away.

Using her sweetest charm, she batted her eyelashes and said, "Did you want me to bring the snake to make for your dinner?"

Malcom stopped and turned back towards them. "While you may think this is a joke, traveling across the country in the midst of Indian territory is no laughing matter."

Haley swallowed the lump in her throat.

"Thanks to your endeavors, they now know we're here."

Macey gasped, covering her mouth with her hand as her face turned pale.

Regret washed over Haley as her eyes moistened. She nodded and grabbed her pail of berries, not saying a word for fear she would break down in tears.

Chapter Three

*A*s *they sat around the campfire,* Malcom watched as the single fellas fawned over Haley and her cooking. She'd outdone herself on her first official meal on the trail. The stew had smooth gravy, and her biscuits were indescribable.

"What's on these?" Malcom held up a partially eaten biscuit for her to see.

"Whatever it is, it's scrumptious." Skip Anderson plopped the rest of his biscuit in his mouth and licked his fingers. "Mind if I have another, ma'am?"

"It's butter mixed with a bit of cinnamon and honey." Haley smiled. "By all means, go ahead and have another."

Malcom was glad she allowed him to get his own instead of waiting on them all hand and foot. She had to be tired from the long day's journey, and then preparing such a delicious meal.

"Don't forget to save some of those biscuits for the trail tomorrow because you're not eating any of our share," Colby said. "Them vittles are well worth fighting for." He gave Haley a toothy grin.

If she continued to cook like this, his work crew wasn't likely to go join any of the other wagons for a meal. Not to mention, Haley was a sight for sore eyes.

"I must admit, I can't believe a woman as handsome as yourself, who can cook this good, isn't married." Galen Marshfield was the only single fella who didn't work for Malcom. He was a cattle rancher with his father. Thanks to him, they were provided milk from some of the cows he'd brought along, and the promise of a cow to celebrate when they completed their journey. "I'm sorry. I've embarrassed you."

She shook her head. "Thank you for your kind words, but I'm recently widowed."

"I'm sorry," Galen said.

The other men all looked at her with solemn faces. Malcom wanted to change the subject but didn't know what to say. He'd found it hard to talk with anyone about being a widower himself.

"Do you have other kinfolk?" Galen's words were gentle, but Malcom felt it wasn't his place to pry.

Of course, Malcom had asked her the same question that morning.

"My parents are back in Britain." Haley picked at her biscuit, nibbling small bites as she spoke. "My husband and I never had any children, so the only kin I have here is my brother and his family. That's why I joined the wagon train, so I can find them."

"You don't know where they are?" Colby asked.

"They were at Fort Bent the last time that I received correspondence from them." Haley stared into the fire embers, her hands paused in their task. "But that has been months."

Their lingering silence drew her attention. "I'm sorry. I don't mean to be so depressing. How about dessert?"

"You keep cooking like this and one of the young bucks is gonna sweep you off your feet," Skip said.

Malcom frowned. Skip was nearing fifty and should have had enough sense to not pressure a new widow about getting remarried. Women with children often remarried to have someone to look out for them, and perhaps Haley would eventually remarry. But losing your family didn't mean you were ready to replace them—at least he wasn't.

Haley busied herself with placing dessert on tin plates for each of them. Malcom's chest tightened when he took his from her. Blueberry cobbler. The same berries she'd risked her life earlier that day to retrieve. He took a bite, trying to be polite, but it felt like he was eating fish bones. The way the others were devouring theirs in heaping spoonsful told him it was just him having trouble.

The long trail rides were always guaranteed to see trouble, even death. But being the first day, he hadn't expected to face trouble so quickly. Men knew the dangers they faced. Women and children needed someone to look out for them. His position as leader meant he was responsible for all of their lives.

Preoccupied with his inner demons, Malcom hadn't noticed Haley approach until she sat down on the log next to him.

"You don't like the cobbler?"

"It's not that." He set the tin plate down between them and folded his hands together as he leaned on his thighs. "While I appreciate your efforts, I can't help but think what might have happened to you today."

"I know." Haley sniffed. "I didn't mean to put everyone in danger." A moment of silence lingered. "Do you really think we could have trouble with Indians?"

"We've generally done our best to avoid any that may have been deemed hostile, and some we've traded within the past…" Malcom shrugged. "But there have been some recent problems."

"Have you encountered trouble with them on your journeys?"

"That's hard to answer." Malcom took a deep breath and expelled it slowly. "I had received word that my wife and children were killed by Indians in February when I was headed back from Santa Fe. I decided not to take a group back to Independence, so I could deal with the matter. The men opted to stay with me. We later learned the wagon train had been attacked by Indians and there were no survivors."

Haley gasped. She laid her hand on his arm. "I'm sorry, Malcom."

The sun was setting lower on the horizon. He looked at her hand on his forearm. It had been a long time since he'd felt the warmth of human contact. He'd gripped her arm earlier, but it wasn't a gentle, comforting touch like now.

"I should have been there for my family." His voice was hoarse.

"You couldn't know, and even if you were there, chances are you would have died too."

Even though he didn't want to admit it, she was right.

"I can't do anything about what happened." Malcom cleared his throat. "But I can do my best to keep everyone else safe. Which means asking you to be careful. Don't wander off without letting me know."

"I promise." Haley crossed her heart, something she had a habit of doing when agreeing to something. "And I'll do my best to talk with you if I have any concerns or need any help."

"Thank you. I appreciate that." Malcom picked up his plate of blueberry cobbler and took a bite. "This really is very good."

Chapter Four

Nearing Comanche Territory — June 27, 1840

Haley usually welcomed Macey's companionship when her parents allowed her to ride with Haley to keep her company, but today Macey was a chatterbox.

"Do you think we'll run into any Indians?" Macey wrung her hands, her gaze flitted across the horizon. "I overheard my pa talking to Skip. He told Pa that Comanche killed Mr. Wheeler's kin and attacked a wagon train. Did you even know Mr. Wheeler had a missus and kids?"

She was starting to prefer the rambling as opposed to Macey's questions. "I think Malcom prefers to not talk about it." Haley slowed the horses to go over some bumpy terrain. "Which I totally understand. It brings up painful memories."

"I noticed you always refer to him by his given name." Macey eyed her. "And neither he nor the others refer to you as Missus."

"When I first joined the wagon train, it was hard for me to talk about what I was still going through. I didn't correct anyone to tell them I was widowed so they wouldn't ask what happened or why we didn't have any children." They wouldn't be stopping for a couple hours so Haley decided she might as well bare her soul to Macey. The young girl had questions about life that her mother seemed uncomfortable answering. If Haley could answer those things for Macey, she might as well continue being honest and open with her. Besides, she knew if she didn't answer, Macey had a habit of coming back to it again, even if it was a day or two later. "It's hard being a wife who can't give your husband the one thing he wants—children. I've always felt like a failure, even though my husband never made me feel that way."

"What was your husband like?" Macey asked.

Haley smiled. She was glad to be able to talk about her husband but also thankful it took Macey's mind off the possibility of seeing Indians.

"My Thomas had light brown hair that would turn almost blond in the summer sun." Warmth flooded Haley at the memory. She could almost smell his sweat from memory and see his face smiling down on her. How she longed to feel strong arms around her, comforting her and telling her everything would be all right. "My husband was a farmer and had the kind of muscles you get from working hard all day in the field. Although, since we came to this country after Christmas, we hadn't gotten to go west and settle on our own land. Even a strong man like him never stood a chance against sepsis."

"How long were you both married?"

"Eight years."

"Ma'am." Haley startled. She hadn't noticed Galen Marshfield ride up alongside her wagon. "Malcom said to warn the wagons that we're being watched by Indian scouts. Normally he would want to set up camp here, but he thinks we need to get through their territory as quickly as possible."

Haley nodded. She noticed Galen held his rifle. He expected trouble.

"I'll ride alongside your wagon to make sure you're protected." It was a noble gesture from Galen. She knew he was sweet on her, but he was a couple years younger and more like a kid-brother to her.

"I've got my husband's rifle in back." She handed the reins to Macey. "Take these please." Haley leaned over the back of her seat and dug underneath a cover for the revolver before turning back around. "I'll keep this close." She placed the gun between her and Macey, tucking it beneath her skirt.

Galen was laughing when she took the reins and looked over at him. "Remind me not to make you mad."

"Oh, trust…" Haley chuckled. "You won't do it twice."

"That I won't." Galen winked at her before he tipped his hat to her and maneuvered his horse several feet from her wagon.

"All the fellas seem taken with you," Macey said. "Even Mr. Wheeler."

Macey had insisted she address Malcom formally to show him the respect he deserved as their leader. Haley probably should have set a better example, which was one of her downfalls. Most men didn't appreciate a woman speaking out of turn. She thought about how fired up one of the men had gotten after dinner last night when she'd made a political comment. Malcom had stared the man down which surprisingly put him back in his place.

"It is Mr. Wheeler's place to look out for all of us," Haley said. "We both just happen to share a similar heartache which makes it easier for us to talk with one another about."

"Pa said he never knew Mr. Wheeler to talk so much before his wife died." Macey had a habit for stating facts or at least what she believed something to be.

She was wrong.

She was also too young to understand comradery. That's what Malcom and Haley shared—nothing more.

Malcom hoped to cross at the lowest place he thought was

passible across the Arkansas River in Kansas. The water was down this time of year, but that didn't make it any easier crossing with wagons and livestock. It also meant they could be in more danger with wagons on both sides of the river should the Indians decide to attack.

While Malcom once believed he had a good relationship with the Comanche leader, Chief Raging River, the murder of his family and slaughter of the other wagon train several months ago painted a different story.

Dying didn't scare Malcom. Failing to protect those who'd placed their trust in him did. He'd risk everything to ensure their safety.

Circling the wagons, he put Skip in charge. "I'm going to ride out and meet the scouts. Hopefully Chief Raging River will grant us safe passage."

To help his chances, he gathered canned fruit, a racoon hat and other items he could round up from members of the wagon train. Galen had even given one of his cows as a token of friendship. Malcom hoped the gifts would not be inspiration for the Indians to raid them and take the rest of their supplies.

"Do you really think it's wise to ride out and meet them?" Haley's eyes narrowed. Concern etched her face like sadness. "Maybe someone else should go?"

Skip's eyes widened, nearly causing Malcom to laugh, even if it wasn't a funny matter. He knew the other men didn't feel comfortable around the Indian's, especially after stories of massacres had circulated.

"I'm the only one who can speak their language." Which was true. "It is safer if I go and ask permission to cross their land."

"But…" Haley glanced toward the direction they'd seen the scout last. "You know what they're capable of."

"Which is why I have to go." A knot formed in the pit of his stomach. "Maybe I can get answers?"

Haley stared into his eyes. Her pain reflected his own. She knew his loss and the questions that haunted him. While God hadn't answered directly, encountering the Comanche tribe again might provide him with the closure he so desperately sought.

Unexpectedly, Haley flung her arms around him in a hug. He instinctively embraced her, reveling in the warmth of human contact.

She continued to cling to him. He heard her praying beneath her breath. As hard as he had found it to pray for so long, Haley's insistence of blessing their meals, and then later asking him to pray with her about things had started to melt his icy exterior and soften his heart. His anger toward God hadn't completely gone away but at least now he wasn't afraid to tell God he was angry and why.

Inhaling a deep breath to absorb Haley's scent, he reluctantly released her. "I need to go."

A tear trickled down her cheek as she nodded.

Walking away from Haley, knowing the anguish she felt at possibly loosing him, wrenched his gut. They'd both faced enough loss to last a lifetime. As he mounted his horse and took the rope to lead the cow, he ushered a prayer for protection.

The scout remained perched on his horse. Malcom glanced beyond him and saw other Indians approaching. Their long braids and dark skin were unmistakable. They didn't have war paint on their faces. Although that didn't guarantee they wouldn't be ready for battle. Even though it had been many moons since he'd last seen him, Malcom recognized Chief Raging River.

When they reached the scout, they all rode together to meet Malcom. He greeted them in their native tongue. Their English was not very good, so they continued to speak Uto-Aztecan.

"I wondered when you would return," the chief said. "I see fire still burns in your eyes."

"Yes," Malcom admitted. He was angry. "My family was my world."

Chief Raging River nodded. "And you believe the picture they painted for you to see?"

Malcom was confused. "What picture?"

"Your family and the wagon train."

"The picture of them?" Malcom struggled to make sense of the chief's words. There was only so much you could translate and comprehend within the two languages. The chief had once called him *the man of many words* because it took so long to explain things.

"Man sees what he wants to see," the chief said. "If you open your eyes and look closer, you will see what is really there."

It felt like a riddle. Malcom had the feeling that the chief wanted him to go and look at things again. Something wasn't right. Chief Raging River was saying that things weren't always what they appeared to be.

"I will go and see." Malcom nodded. "I have brought you gifts."

The chief's son rode closer to take the items that Malcom had brought. He handed him the cow. "I hope the milk will warm your children's bellies."

Rising Moon thanked him.

Malcom turned his attention back to the chief. "May we have permission to travel across Comanche land?"

The chief gave his blessing. "The Comanche wish to keep peace with you. We have traded many moons. Others wish to stop this and bring about war."

"Others? Who are they?"

"Men with greed in their eyes and anger in their hearts," Chief Raging River said. "They do not think twice to kill their own."

Chapter Five

Beside Arkansas River in Kansas — June 28, 1840

*S*unday service had concluded with songs of praise. Then menfolk asked for a meeting after church. They'd apparently appointed Reverend Durwood to speak on their behalf. He'd seen to it that the women went about tending to the children so that the men could speak in private. Malcom continued to sit on his log near Haley and whittled a piece of wood with his knife.

"I know the Lord says we shall not fear," Reverend Durwood said, "but it is up to us to look out for the women and children, even the widows such as Missus Hunter."

"Speaking of which, she should be with the other womenfolk." William Hendershot was a crotchety old man who believed women and children should be seen and not heard.

"She represents her household." Malcom's tone was firm. "She can stay if she wishes."

William started to say something else but halted at the narrowed gaze Malcom shot him. He swished his chewing tobacco to the side of his mouth and spit on the ground.

"As I was saying," Reverend Durwood continued, "many of us have concern about the Indians. What guarantee do we have that they will not attack?"

"About the same chance of it raining tomorrow." Malcom knew he was being sarcastic. "You yourself have preached before that no one has been guaranteed tomorrow. In fact, I'm pretty sure you said that at the last funeral I heard you preach."

"While that may be true…" Reverend Durwood cleared his throat. "The Lord never told Daniel to put his head inside the lion's mouth."

"I heard they are planning to send soldiers to deal with them filthy—"

"Enough." Malcom cut off Macey's father, Marcus. Irritation rose in him faster than the temperature on a hot day. "You all knew the risk associated with traveling across the country before you joined." Malcom expelled a deep breath. "Chief Raging River has assured me that his tribe has not been behind any of the attacks."

"And you trust an Indian?" Marcus asked.

"Their word is their bond." Which was more than he could say about some men he knew. "The Chief also offered to send escorts with me and some men to look over the wagon train's remains."

"Are you sure it isn't a plan to separate us and attack?" William asked.

"If they had wanted to kill us," Malcom said, "we would already be dead."

"Are you going to go with them?" Reverend Durwood's brow furrowed.

"Yes." Malcom straightened. "And I thought you'd go with me. Then you can pray over the dead." If they were dying, he thought it was considered last rights. He didn't really know what they called it when the person wasn't alive.

The pastor frowned but nodded his head. He almost laughed at the thought of someone finally guilting a preacher to do something instead of the other way around.

"While we're gone, the rest of you should go over the

wagons. Check the wheels and make sure they're sturdy or make repairs necessary."

"It's Sunday," Reverend Durwood said. "It should be a day of rest."

"That it should." Malcom stood and put his knife back in its sheath. "But I figured if everyone was concerned about how long we camped here, then maybe we should take the time to prepare so we can leave after breakfast tomorrow." Malcom was anxious to leave behind his bad memories but curious to find out what really happened.

"I believe the Good Lord would forgive us this one indiscretion." Reverent Durwood held up his Bible. "In times of need, Jesus healed on the sabbath. I do declare He would consider this a time of need."

Within half-an-hour, Malcom and the preacher were on their way. Chief Raging River had sent his son, Running Bull, and another Indian to guide them.

Running Bull laughed about the preacher following in a wagon while they rode on horseback.

Malcom chuckled too and told them he wasn't sure if the pastor knew how to ride a horse. He didn't tell them Reverend Durwood hoped to find any of the people's mementos and return them to their families. Malcom knew as well as Running Bull did that anything of value would have been taken in the raid and everything else torched.

They saw the wagons before they even reached the site. One of them had a partially burnt canvas on it still. His stomach felt tighter than dried up leather. As they drew closer, he spotted graves marked by sticks formed in the shape of crosses. There were a lot of them. Enough to make him want to lose the lunch he'd eaten a couple hours earlier.

He and the others dismounted, tying the horses to a wagon. The pastor joined them moments later.

"What do you see when you look around?" Running Bull made a sweeping motion with his arm, indicating the remains of the attack.

"What did he say?" Reverend Durwood glanced from their

guides back to him.

"He wants to know what we see?"

"Is he blind?" The preacher frowned. "We see the same thing he sees. Except we didn't get to see the bodies before they were buried so we can't be for sure if they were scalped."

"They were scalped," Running Bull said in English.

Both men turned to stare at him. Malcom didn't know he spoke their language.

"So, they were killed by Indians," Reverend Durwood's tone was matter-of-fact.

"Indians learned to scalp by the white man." Running Bull glared at the pastor. "White men leave tracks."

"He's not making any sense, and he's speaking blasphemy," Reverend Durwood said. "I've never heard of any white men scalping."

"Yet you speak of the Devil and have not seen him."

"He's got you there." Malcom smirked. "By your own words, you can't claim that Satan is real if you haven't seen him."

"How does he even know about the Devil?" Reverend Durwood spoke in a lower voice, eyeing Running Bull suspiciously.

"You are not the first man to come and tell us about your god."

"He's everyone's God, if they will let Him be." Reverend Durwood had assumed his pulpit voice when defending his beliefs.

"Even the god of the men who did this?" Running Bull spread his arms out, indicating the scene they were examining.

"Well…" Reverend Durwood stammered. "He obviously wasn't their God, but He will be their judge and will make sure they pay for what they've done."

They were lucky that God would be their judge, or even a regular judge, because he would do more than just hang them for what they'd done. Why should they get any better punishment than what they'd bestowed on their victims? They deserved to suffer—and die a hundred deaths!

Malcom scoured the area. There were ashes from a campfire, so the wagon train had spent the night here. That meant it wasn't a sudden attack in which they rounded up the wagons for protection.

There were cowboy boot tracks that had dried in the mud. Spotting something sticking up out of the dried dirt, Malcom bent down. He wiggled the metal back and forth, then used his index finger to move some of the dirt around it to retrieve what turned out to be a detailed spur. Someone had this special made.

"I found a trunk," Reverend Durwood said. He was struggling to remove it from the underneath of one of the wagons. Whoever torched the group must not have noticed it or they would have taken it in the raid.

Another thing Malcom noticed was that all of the horse hooves tracks were from shoed horses—something the Indian's didn't ride. They could have been on horses they'd stolen from white men before. As hard as it was to admit, Malcom was starting to understand Chief Raging River's revelation. But why would someone want this to look like an Indian attack? And what type of people would be capable of killing innocent settlers?

Chapter Six

*H*áley *stared at the contents in the* back of the wagon. The engraved floral trunk was a family heirloom. If they found it at the massacre, it only meant one thing—they were dead. Her mind struggled to grasp things. They were supposed to send for her. This wagon train was headed back to Independence. So why would they have been with them? She was going to be joining them. So was Thomas. She had sent word about him. Maybe that's why they were heading back? If so, was it her fault they had been killed?

"Do you know if there were any survivors?" Her voice sounded hoarse. Speaking strained her throat. Stomach acids churned, threatening to erupt as sweat beaded her brow.

"What's wrong?" Panic etched Malcom's voice.

She looked at him. "That's my family's trunk." A tear trickled down her cheek. "Did anyone live?"

He closed his eyes a moment before slowly shaking his head. "I'm sorry."

As Haley broke down in uncontrollable sobs, Malcom's strong arms wrapped around her and held her. Her mind whirled with grief, followed with questions. Losing her family was painful enough but then another realization hit her. There were few choices for a woman on her own in this strange land. How would she get by? "Where am I going to go?"

"We'll think of something." Malcom gently stroked her back.

Maybe he'd be willing to let her continue to cook on the wagon train? But how long could she keep up with always moving around? Did she always want to worry about being attacked by Indians? What kind of life was that?

Haley wiped the tears from her eyes and took a step away from Malcom. She'd take time to pray for guidance. "I'm sorry. You must think me foolish."

"Not in the least." His voice was husky. "I'm here for you if you need anything."

"Thank you." Haley gave him a swift hug. "Did you find out what happened to them?"

"They were all buried, with stick crosses marking their graves." Malcom looked deeply into her eyes as if he were boring into her very soul. He knew her pain—he'd felt it when he lost his family. "Chief Raging River was right that things aren't as they appear."

"What do you mean?" Haley's chest tightened. She covered her heart with her hand. "Who else would have done that to them?"

"I don't know, but I intend to find out."

She wanted whoever did this to pay for their sins. But the mindset of someone who could do such a thing was barbaric. If it wasn't Indians, then how many people did it take to do this? "Be careful. You don't know who they are and if you go around asking questions it could put you in danger."

"That's why I've asked the reverend to keep this between us for now," Malcom said. "When we get to the fort, I'll speak with whoever is in charge. Hopefully they will look into things."

"I won't mention it with anyone." She wanted him to be safe.

"Thank you." Malcom gave her a warm smile. "Would you like me to have someone carry the trunk to your wagon?"

"Yes." Haley appreciated his thoughtfulness. "I can get some leftovers together for you to eat while you're taking care of that."

Malcom nodded, giving her arm a little squeeze as he passed by.

When they pulled up camp on Monday morning, Malcom insisted on riding with Haley because he knew she was still grieving the loss of her kin. He also worried whether she would be able to guide the horses in crossing the river with the wagon. The wagons lined up to cross. Malcom insisted on taking Haley's across first so that he could come back and help with the others.

Malcom instructed Skip and Eli to ride their horses across so that they could find the best path to take the wagons and cattle. Once they found the spot they thought was the safest, they started to cross with her wagon. Haley braced herself, holding on to her seat, afraid to grab Malcom's arm. She wanted to make sure he had the freedom to guide the horses in their task.

The horses were quickly covered to their underbellies in water. Haley realized she was holding her breath and biting her lip as they crossed. If water got into the back of the wagon, her flour and other food items would get wet and ruined.

Making clicking noises, Malcom encouraged the horses as they huffed to pull the wagon through the water. The wagon felt like it started to float at one point, but Malcom guided the horses to keep it from turning and pulling them downstream. Once they returned to dry ground, Haley expelled a long breath.

"Whoa." Malcom brought the horse and wagon to a stop

near some trees. "You should be okay here while I finish helping to get the others across."

"Thank you." She took the reins from him and laid them on the seat.

While Malcom did that, Haley retrieved her sister-in-law's journal that she'd found in the chest last night. She didn't have enough daylight to read her entries. Now would be a good opportunity, plus it would take her mind off of Malcom and the others crossing. Water made her nervous. One of the boys from her class had drowned when they were younger. His empty seat always made her sad and seeing water closeup made her think of what it must have been like to be surrounded by it with no way to breath. Her heart quickened just thinking about the scenario.

She retrieved the journal and sat on the wagon bench, brushing a hand over the two-tone leather. As she flipped through the pages, she realized Sarah had begun the journal years ago, when she and Joshua had married. Sarah's entries were not daily. There were many events listed, like the birth of their two children. Haley smiled reading them as she remembered the days. Sarah had also made note of how her heart ached for Haley not having any children and how wonderful of a mother she thought Haley would be.

Sadness washed over Haley. With little options for a woman, if Malcom didn't continue to let her work as a cook on his wagon train excursions, she would either be forced to remarry, or she would have to find a way to come up with the money for the voyage back to Britain.

"Why the frown?"

Haley jumped. Her gaze darted to Galen.

"Sorry, I didn't mean to scare you." He smiled, a bit of playfulness lit up his eyes. "By your smile, I hope that means you're happy to see me?"

Her grin widened. Galen always had a way of putting people at ease. "Of course, I'm glad to see you but it's not like you ever left."

"True." Galen cocked his head to the side. "But it does seem a little difficult to get you alone."

Was he flirting with her? Galen was unmarried and considerably handsome with blond hair and blue eyes. She was two years older than him, not that a couple years made that big of a difference. "Might I ask your reason for wanting to get me alone?"

He chuckled. "I like a woman who is direct."

Galen leaned forward, resting his head on top of his hands on the sideboard of the wagon.

The sun must have risen considerably higher in the sky because Haley's cheeks warmed.

He seemed to notice her uncomfortableness and smiled even wider. "You sure are pretty."

Haley's gaze locked with his. He was flirting. She was flattered. But did she feel that way about him?

"We're about ready to go." Malcom's presence startled her. He didn't look happy.

"Is everything okay?" Haley's heart raced. She noticed the scowl on Malcom's face when he glanced at Galen. She should have asked Malcom in private.

Malcom didn't answer. Instead, he rode his horse around to the rear of the wagon and dismounted, tying his horse to the back of her wagon again.

"Looks like our father is back. We best be careful or we're likely to get in trouble." Galen winked at her. "You've got options, Haley. Just make sure to keep them open and give me a chance."

Chapter Seven

Monday, June 29, 1840

Malcom didn't have the right to be angry but he was infuriated. Haley was a grown woman and shouldn't have been acting like a silly school girl. The fact that she was taken in by Galen's charms shouldn't have eaten at his craw, but it did.

"I'm sorry. I shouldn't have asked you if there was a problem in front of anyone."

He glanced over at Haley before focusing on the trail. "It doesn't matter."

"Obviously it does since you're still angry."

Women. That's why she thought he was upset? "That's not why I'm upset."

"Then why are you upset?" she asked. "Did I do something else wrong?"

He shook his head, debating whether or not to say more. Silence lingered in the air. Malcom thought about the last time he'd been upset with Sara. She had actually been the one angry with him for being gone so long. He should have been there for her—listened to her concerns more.

"I'm concerned about you being vulnerable right now."

There, he said it.

Haley giggled.

Malcom eyes darted toward her. "What's so funny?"

"So, he was flirting with me?" She continued to find amusement in that revelation for some reason.

"And it looked like you welcomed his attention." Which is what really rubbed him the wrong way.

"I was flattered." She stared at him. "If I didn't know better, I'd think you were jealous."

"And what if I am?"

She opened her mouth to say something, then closed it.

They rode in stunned silence. Horses snorting mixed with the sound of the wagon wheels and bumping across dry ground wafted through the air. Malcom couldn't believe he'd made such a revelation. In fact, he hadn't even realized he felt that way.

He worried his words may have caused an uncomfortable rift between them. At least now she knew his intentions, and so did he. Malcom hadn't ever dreamed of getting married again after what happened to his family. Not that being attracted to someone meant you would end up marrying them. But letting Haley know his interest in her at least gave her something to think about so that she wouldn't go rushing into Galen's arms.

Haley was thumbing through the journal in her hands.

"Did you find anything interesting?"

She glanced at him. "Yes, I was reading some of my sister-in-law, Sarah's lasts post."

"What did she have to say?"

"She said she met someone named Sara, but their name didn't have an *h* after it like hers."

"That's how my wife's name was spelled."

Haley looked at him curiously. "I know and I kind of think she is the woman my brother's wife was talking about."

It was his turn to give her a peculiar look. "Why's that?"

"She mentioned David and Michael, which I recall you saying were the names of your sons."

Malcom's breath caught. His chest tightened. He forced

himself to focus on his task, wanting more than anything to stop and read her words for himself.

"What else did she say?" His voice was hoarse.

"She said their children got along well with your sons. She said Sara spoke highly of her husband who made a long journey for supplies and how he would always stop and get her special chocolates on his journey back." Haley's cheeks turned rosy.

"What?" He knew there was something else she wasn't saying.

Haley cleared her throat and moistened her lips. "She said Sara told her that you always said nothing tasted sweeter than her kisses."

Heat rose in Malcom's face. He did love kissing his wife, but she was gone. It was embarrassing to just admit to someone else that you were interested in them, to have them find out things about you from someone else.

When he glanced at Haley, she was smiling. "What?"

"It's all right to remember the feelings you had for your wife," Haley said. "If you recall, I was married as well."

He nodded. That was one of the things that drew them both together—the loss of their spouses.

"She also mentioned some men whom they came across that were asking about Sara's husband." Haley frowned. "Sarah said they were men from a trading company. She didn't like them, said they asked a lot of questions, like how many people were with them. She also said something about how the one had fancy spurs."

Malcom's grip tightened on the reins. "Did she say anything else about them?"

Haley shook her head. "No. She only said she was happy when they were gone and then she wrote about some other stuff a day or two later."

She thumbed back through some of the pages. The color drained from her face.

Malcom slowed the horses and stopped. He turned to Haley. "What?"

"Sara was pregnant."

"Your brother's wife was going to have another baby?" he asked, unsure why that would have impacted her any more than already dealing with their deaths.

"Your Sara." A tear trickled down her face.

He stared numbly at her.

"Is something wrong?" Skip hollered as he rode up to the wagon to check on them. "Why'd you stop?"

"Let everyone take a few minutes to stretch their legs, maybe get something to eat," Malcom mumbled. "Then we'll get back on the trail shortly."

When Skip rode away, he realized Haley's hand on his forearm. "I'm sorry."

He closed his eyes and nodded. A tear trickled down his face. "I'll find whoever did this and make them pay."

"Do you think whoever killed your family also attacked the wagon train?"

"I'd almost bet on it." But he didn't understand why.

Chapter Eight

*A*fter dinner, Macey joined Haley and the unmarried men around the campfire to talk. She caught Galen staring at her several times and even noticed him wink.

Macey wanted to catch the attention of Colby. She joined Haley on several occasions in order to get a glimpse of him. Her efforts hadn't gone unnoticed by the group of men either. Which was why Haley had suggested Macey be more aloof. Sitting next to Haley instead of trying to sit by Colby hadn't exactly been what she had in mind. Men liked to do the pursuing.

"I heard my parents talking," Macey said. "They said you should respond to one of those advertisements for a bride." She chanced a glance toward Colby. "I'm thinking about replying to one of them. After all, it couldn't hurt to write one of the men to get to know them."

Why were her parents talking about her?

"Haley does not need to marry some stranger." Galen's eyebrow arched. "She need look no further than here."

"You sure can cook, Miss Haley." Riley Duncan took his

hat off and held it over his heart. "If you need a husband, I'd be right proud to make you my missus."

Malcom choked on his drink. Stood and tossed the rest of the contents of his coffee on the fire before striding off.

"I admit I am not sure what I am going to do. But thank you all for giving me something to think about." Haley set her tin cup down next to the log and went after Malcom.

She found him less than fifty feet from camp, leaning against a tree, staring at the sunset. He straightened when he heard her coming.

Haley stopped, hands on her hips, and stared quietly at him.

"If you keep looking at me like that I might kiss you."

A smile crept up on her face. "Is that your backwards way of asking my permission?"

He took a step forward, moving within arm's reach of her. Her heart raced, wondering if he would.

His eyes searched hers.

"What about Galen, Riley, or any of the others?" His voice was husky.

"What about them?" She shrugged.

"You'd have a chance at a normal life with any of them. Especially someone like Galen." Malcom flinched. "He comes from a family of means."

"And that means nothing to me." Money was never important. It wouldn't keep her bed warm at night or hold and comfort her when she cried—Malcom would. She knew because he had on several occasions. "But the one thing that may matter to you is having children." Her voice cracked. "I'm not sure I can have children. At least I haven't been able to conceive thus far."

He closed the gap between them, his hands going to her waist to draw her close.

"I know." Malcom leaned his forehead against hers, causing the brim of his hat to brush her head and push it back.

She grinned.

"You have the most adorable dimples." He tilted his head and kissed each one before pausing. His breathing was ragged.

He searched her eyes, which quickly focused in anticipation on his lips. They claimed hers in an exciting dance of embers igniting beneath the intensity.

When their lips parted, they were both breathing heavy. She remembered what it was like to feel such passion and obviously so had he. Haley's body longed to be complete again.

"Perhaps the preacher will hitch us tonight?"

Haley laughed and hugged him before sighing. "It appears I'm not the only one concerned about our need to reign in our desire."

"You're not a woman to mince words." He winked at her. "That's one of the things I admire most about you."

"Maybe we should join the others?" Haley said. "All this sweet talk is going to get us in trouble. Especially standing so close."

A guttural sound escaped Malcom's throat. "Just one more kiss."

That *one* kiss was long and lingering, with a promise of more to come.

Malcom did talk to the preacher and they agreed to wait until Sunday for him to marry them. Reverend Durwood thought it best to sleep on it a few nights and make sure it was what they really wanted.

Part of Haley wondered if the pastor suggested they wait because he thought Haley needed more time to consider her options.

She knew her options and she knew what she wanted—to marry Malcom.

Haley was finishing loading up her wagon when Macey strolled over.

"Good morning." Macey was chipper as usual.

"It was," Haley said, biting her tongue to keep from adding, *until you strolled over.*

"I thought maybe I could ride with you today?" Macey rocked on her heels, her hands folded in front of her.

Haley's hands stilled over their task. "I'm not sure that's a good idea."

"Why?" Macey looked at Haley wide-eyed and innocent.

"You put me in an awkward position last night," Haley said, "not to mention telling me that you and your parents are talking about me behind my back, which isn't very Christian-like."

"I'm sorry." Macey's eyes teared up. "I... I only wanted to bring up the subject of mail order brides to make Caleb think about me as a grown woman who is ready to get married."

"You could have mentioned you were considering it without suggesting that I try it." It was hard for Haley to stay angry with Macey, but she didn't like the position it put her in. "You had all the men looking at me like a charity case and wanting to marry me out of pity."

"Is that why Malcom asked you to marry him?"

Macey's words stung like venom even if she didn't mean them to be harsh. Was that why Malcom proposed? "How do you know he asked me?"

"I heard..." She started to point over her shoulder, then dropped her hand. "I overheard someone gossiping."

Haley's lips pursed together like she'd taken a bite out of a lemon instead of an orange. She stormed off in search of Malcom.

He was on his proverbial high horse when she spotted him, riding around like he was in charge—always Mr. Fix-it. She wasn't a problem to be fixed and wouldn't marry someone out of fake platitudes.

Malcom rode toward her and stopped. His smile faded when he saw her scowl. "What's wrong?"

"I want to talk?"

"Now?" He looked around. "We're getting ready to leave."

"If I didn't want to talk now, would I have bothered to come and find you?" She put her hands on her hips and continued to glare at him.

"Is this our first fight?" Malcom asked, climbing down from

his horse. "Because I would like to get past the arguing and go right to making up. It's so much better."

She wasn't smiling.

His eyes met hers. "What's wrong?"

"Why did you ask me to marry you?" She had to know.

"Because I have strong feelings for you."

"Are you sure you're not just taking pity on me, like the other men?"

Malcom's eyes flung wide open. "You are not some helpless wildflower and you're sure a lot prettier. Honestly, I don't think any of the men showing an interest in you were doing so because they felt sorry for you."

He wasn't saying any words worthy of making a woman swoon. Strong feelings for someone could be any kind of emotion, even anger. "Finding someone pretty or saying they're a good cook is not a declaration of love."

"You're right." Malcom took her in his arms and kissed her senseless. "And come Sunday, I'll be more than happy to stand up and tell the world I love you."

Haley stammered, unsure what to say. She blinked and stared at Malcom.

"Do you think we could go on and get this wagon train on the move?"

She nodded, still speechless.

He winked at her chuckled as he turned and climbed on his horse. Malcom tipped his hat. "I'll see you a little later, future Mrs. Wheeler."

Chapter Nine

Haley and Malcom's Wedding Day, July 5, 1840

$\mathcal{M}$*acey agreed to help Haley prepare* breakfast and assist her in getting ready for her wedding after morning services. "You are very perky this morning, Macey."

"Caleb asked me to sit by him for service today." Macey couldn't stop smiling. "I was hoping to learn how to make the biscuits so that I could tell him that I made them this morning."

"That will be fine," Haley said. "I'll tell you what to do and you do it. That will give me more time to peel potatoes. I thought I would fry some potatoes to go with the smoked ham and biscuits." She wanted a nice meal for her wedding day. Several of the other wagons had offered to help provide something for the afternoon meal so that Haley could relax and enjoy her wedding day.

She wished she would have been able to get to a town to buy a new dress for her wedding. The off-white blouse with a lacy top and collar, paired with a light blue skirt would have to do. Last night, Malcom let her choose the shirt for him today which was a pale blue and white long sleeve plaid shirt.

Preoccupied in her own thoughts, she hadn't realized that Macey was speaking to her. "I'm sorry. My mind's elsewhere right now. What were you saying?"

"That if it wasn't for me suggesting you take out one of those mail order bride advertisements, Malcom may not have come forward and told you his intentions." Macey giggled. "So, in a way, you got together because of me."

It was Haley's turn to laugh. She thought it funny that Macey would try to take credit for them getting together. Like the past month of them eating meals together and talking over dinner had nothing to do with their love blooming. "I hate to rain on your wagon, but Malcom had already told me his feelings the day before."

"Oh." Macey looked like it had just started raining when she planned to go swimming.

Haley silently liked putting the girl in her place. She had a lot to learn, most of which would come with age and experience. "At least it helped to give Caleb a nudge."

Macey perked back up with a smile. Anything concerning Caleb made her grin from ear-to-ear.

"We best get finished with breakfast so that I can get ready for my wedding." Haley gave Macey instructions for how to measure off and mix the ingredients for the biscuits while she sliced potatoes.

Reverend Durwood spoke on marriage and commitment. Haley wished he wouldn't have mentioned it being *until death*. Not because she didn't see herself as always being with Malcom but because it reminded both of them of their loss. She knew that Malcom had expected his marriage to last forever, just as she had but no one had guarantees in life.

She knew there would be obstacles to face and a couple trips on the trail every year. It didn't matter where she was as long as she was with Malcom.

It came to the end of the service and the preacher called them up in front of everyone for the ceremony. Haley took the wild flowers Macey had picked for her. She felt a little funny with the honeysuckles Macey braided in her hair, but a couple of the ladies had commented and said she looked pretty.

Malcom had removed his hat. His smile made her heart race. Glistening green eyes held her captive. Love shone through them, a love she looked forward to sharing, hopefully for a lifetime. She couldn't bear any more loss.

"As you all have heard by now, we are gathered here today for union of Malcom Wheeler and Haley Hunter," Reverend Durwood said.

Several men whooped and hollered. Women sighed or clapped.

The pastor shushed them to gain their attention again. "As a formality, I have to ask if anyone has any reason these two should not be joined in holy matrimony to speak up now or forever hold your peace."

"I reckon I best speak up before it's too late." Galen stood up. Taking his hat off, he clutched the brim in his hands.

Malcom glared at the other man.

"I have come to think fondly of you, as I told you recently." Galen cleared his throat. "However, I did not have the ability to let you know my intentions and properly court you. While Malcom is a fine gentleman, I feel that I can better provide a safe and secure home for you and would be honored if you would consider marrying me instead?"

From the corner of her eye, she saw Malcom clench his fists. She didn't blame him for being upset. She would have been livid if any other woman stood up and asked him to marry them instead. Thankfully, the other women were either married, or younger than Macey.

"I appreciate the offer," Haley said. "But my heart belongs to Malcom." She turned to Malcom. "We both have shared sorrow and understand the pain each other has felt and together we have been able to find true happiness again. I look forward to the days ahead with you, wherever the trail may take us, I'll always be happy as long as you are by my side."

"Those would make some mighty fine wedding vows,"

Reverend Durwood chuckled. "If there are no other objections, then let us begin the wedding ceremony." He perused the group. No one uttered any other protest, so he continued with marrying Malcom and Haley.

When he pronounced them married and told Malcom he could kiss the bride, her heart strummed a marry beat to the music and cheering that erupted. She melted into Malcom as his kiss turned her insides to butter.

The guttural sound he made echoed the desire she felt for him as well. Come tonight, she would truly be his wife. She longed for the two becoming one flesh.

Dancing and celebrating rang out as several other couples were prompted by the remembrance of the vows they had once made. It was a time of celebration for all. Even Galen, who asked her to dance. Malcom had gracefully allowed her to.

"I'm sorry for putting a damper on your wedding day." Galen was apologetic. He looked contrite. "You are a wonderful woman and I know Malcom realizes how blessed he is to have you."

"I'm equally blessed to have him." Haley smiled. "God knew we both had shared loss and could comfort each other. Our time of sorrow has turned to rejoicing."

Galen nodded. "I understand that now."

"I will pray for you," Haley said, "that God sends you a wife who will make you feel complete."

"Thank you."

"You might want to pray as well," Haley teased. "It never hurts to put your order in with the Creator. Let Him know what you are looking for in a wife."

"I may have to make a list." They both laughed.

"May I cut in?" Malcom asked.

"By all means," Galen said. "You are definitely a blessed man."

Galen stepped aside, and Malcom took his place. "Don't I know it."

The day's events had been tiring and emotional. As the camp settled down with the setting sun, Malcom led Haley to the tent that had been pitched for them. Tonight, the two would be joined in holy matrimony—their nights would no longer be lonely.

Chapter Ten

Fort Bent, July 28, 1840

*F*ort *Bent stretched in front of them* like a welcoming drink after a draught. Malcom counted himself blessed to have made the trip without any casualties. Especially happy to have found himself a wife. The very thought made him smile.

Although he was very thankful, he still had not given up on pursuing justice for his late wife or for Haley's family who had been murdered.

When they arrived at the fort, Malcom quickly found Haley. He helped her down from the wagon and tied the reins up to one of the posts. "We need to find the ranking officer."

Malcom stopped one of the enlisted men and found directions, along with the name of the head officer—Lt. Col. Declan McGuire.

"Excuse me, miss," a gruff man with a beard said as he tipped his hat to pass Haley. Two other men followed behind him, allowing them to pass.

Giving the middle-aged man the once over, Malcom's attention rested on his boots, and the missing spur. "Pardon me." Malcom cleared his throat. "I wonder if I might have a word with you?"

He leaned forward to whisper in Haley's ear, "Go find the lieutenant colonel and bring him immediately."

She gave him a peculiar look but nodded and hurried off.

"What seems to be the problem?" The man's question was not asked neighborly. His two sidekicks sensed trouble, standing erect on either side of him. Not a one of them appeared to have seen a drop of water in weeks. They smelled ripe.

"I noticed your boots." Malcom looked toward them. "Those are some fancy spurs you have—appears you're missing one of them."

He raised his heel and frowned. "Looks like I'll need to get a new one made. Good thing there's a guy here who can take care of it."

"That's good to know." Malcom realized he was grinding his teeth. He took a deep breath. "Does he make a lot of the same design on the spurs?"

"No," the guy said. "They're all one of a kind. That's why he said he charges so much for them."

"Hey, did you happen to visit that wagon train that was massacred a few months back?"

That caught all three of their attention.

"Can't say that I did." He tipped his hat. "We best be going."

"Hold up," Malcom said. "I still have a couple questions for you."

Haley returned with two soldiers.

"I'm Lt. Col. Declan McGuire." He glanced from the other men to Malcom. "Your Missus says you needed to speak with me urgently."

"Yes." Although Malcom had more on his mind than mere words. "I have reason to believe these men were behind a wagon train massacre and were also responsible for killing my first wife."

The three accused looked startled as their eyes widened, the one with the missing spur's eyes narrowed. "That's some pretty hefty accusations."

Malcom glared at him before addressing the lieutenant colonel. "Which I can assure you I can back up with proof."

"I already told you we weren't anywhere near that wagon train." His angry tone didn't convince Malcom of his proclaimed innocence.

"Then how did your spur end up there?" Malcom pulled the spur in question from his pocket. "And we found a journal from one of the slain women who also mentioned you. As you said yourself, the man who makes these spurs doesn't believe in making duplicates, he only does *one of a kind* I believe your exact words were."

Lt. Col. Declan McGuire took the spur from Malcom and examined it. He glanced at the man's boots. "I'll have to ask the three of you to come along with me."

They started to turn and run, but a couple other soldiers were approaching.

Malcom wanted to shoot them, but with his wife near, he didn't want to risk her getting hurt if things became violent.

The soldiers removed the weapons from the three men and escorted them back to the lieutenant colonel's headquarters.

Malcom stared down into his wife's teary eyes. "Go and get your sister-in-law's journal and bring it back to us." He wiped away a tear that trickled down her cheek. "We'll see that these men pay for what they did."

Haley hugged him briefly before she went off to do as she was bid. Malcom hurried to catch up to the officer who was waiting for him.

"Do you have any idea as to why they would have done these heinous acts?" Lt. Col. McGuire asked.

"They were apparently targeting me because they were asking questions about me when they visited the wagon train. I would have been there had my wife and children not been murdered." The pain still ate at him. "I don't know why they wanted to make it look like a Comanche raid unless they were just trying to get away with it and wanted to throw suspicion on the Indians."

"We'll soon find out." Lieutenant Colonel McGuire was a seasoned man and carried himself with the authority he'd earned.

The soldiers seated the three accused men in chairs in front of the lieutenant colonel's desk.

Lt. Col. McGuire stood behind his desk, hands behind his back, and sternly glared at each of the men.

"We already have proof that you were at the wagon train." He tossed the spur that Malcom had given him onto his desk. "There's evidence and I'm sure that we can have Buckley come over and verify that it is the same spur that he made for you. The only thing I've yet to understand is why you would do something like this?"

"We weren't with him," the thin, lanky man of the group said.

"Shut up." He spit, not the least bit concerned that they were inside, or whether or not he hit one of the soldier's boots.

"We were just following orders," the other one offered. "Joshua Stanton hired us."

Haley returned with the journal. She brought it over to McGuire and opened it to the entry regarding the entry in question.

"Why did Joshua Stanton target me and my family?" Malcom asked.

"He felt you were messing up his business by bringing in other traders instead of just settlers," the stockier of the three said. "He thought for sure losing your family would deter you and when it didn't, he told us to make it look like an Indian raid, so it would deter others from traveling the path you took."

"He thought people would be superstitious and think you were bad luck," the lanky man added.

"Why don't the two of you shut up?" Malcom knew the man missing the spur was upset because they had him dead-to-rights.

"With what is written in this journal and your spur that was found at the massacre, we have enough to hold you for the murders," Lt. Col. McGuire said. "All we have left to do is apprehend Joshua Stanton."

Chapter Eleven

Santa Fe, New Mexico, August 11, 1840

Malcom left Haley behind at Fort Bent under the supervision of Lt. Col. Declan McGuire in order to go with the other soldiers on horseback to Santa Fe and apprehend Joshua Stanton. Leaving her behind was one of the toughest things he'd had to do, but it was safer for her. You could never trust how a cornered man would react. A dozen men had been spared for this journey.

He'd had the past two weeks to think about life, not just wanting vengeance. This was the first time in their marriage that he and Haley had been apart. The intensity in which he missed her weighed on him like a millstone. He'd be happy when this was all over with.

They arrived at Santa Fe two weeks later, on a Tuesday. It wasn't an area that Malcom liked as much because of being dry and hot. He liked the places that had lush, green grass and regular trees instead of cactus plants. Not that some cactus couldn't be pretty if they had flowers that bloomed on them.

The men that Joshua Stanton had hired told Lt. Col. McGuire of a ranch that Stanton owned. When he arrived with the military, the place appeared to be well fortified. Four men on horseback greeted them at the entryway to the property. The lead officer handed one of the men a scrolled letter from McGuire.

The Mexican handed it back. "You don't have authority here. This is private property"

"Joshua Stanton is wanted for crimes he ordered to be committed," the soldier said. "We have orders to bring him in dead or alive. Whether or not you choose to join him is up to you."

He nodded. "I will take you to him, senor."

They followed him up a long road to the ranch. Malcom was well aware that they were being watched from the distance. There were stables not far from the house. Plenty of room for them to hide if they decided to ambush them.

A man in a suit, toting a gold pocket watch, strolled out into the courtyard. Presumably Joshua Stanton. "How may I help you gentlemen?"

"We have orders to take you in for questioning Mr. Stanton," the officer said as he got down off his horse, removed his riding glove, and handed Mr. Stanton his scrolled letter.

Joshua read it and returned the paper to the officer. "I'm sure this is just a misunderstanding."

"Then come with us and we can get it straightened out." The officer's eyes never left Joshua.

"And if I refuse?" Joshua's eyebrow quirked. For whatever reason, he seemed amused.

Malcom didn't trust him.

"Trust me when I say, you'd rather come with us," Malcom said. "If the Comanche find you, they'll scalp you."

"And why would they do that," he asked, "besides the fact that they're wild savages?"

"They know you had my family and the wagon train killed and made it look like them."

That drew a startled look from Joshua.

"It wouldn't surprise me if they decided to show up here and give you a personal demonstration of how it should be done."

Malcom forced himself to remain calm and aloof, even though every part of him wanted to draw his weapon and remove the sorry excuse for a man from the planet. Everyone would understand. Any man would want justice for his family. The only thing that stopped him were scriptures reminding him that God was his judge, not Malcom.

"What makes you think I would be any safer traveling to the fort with you then?" Joshua asked.

"Because Chief Raging River is a friend and he knows how much I've lost," Malcom said. "He would be the first to say it is my place to bring you to justice or kill you. Either one works for me, so if you don't wish to come with us, I'd be happy to save the chief the trouble of coming after you."

Chapter Twelve

Fort Bent, August 25, 1840

*H*aley didn't know if either the food or the water wasn't agreeing with her. She had been on edge since Malcom left four weeks ago. He was due back any day. She decided to go see the fort's doctor in case anything she had may be contagious.

Standing outside his door, she hesitated before knocking. The last time she'd had anything to do with a doctor was when her first husband was dying of sepsis.

"Come in," Doctor Adams said in a raised tone.

"Hello," Haley said as she entered the room.

The doctor was bandaging up a soldier's hand. "I'll be with you in a moment."

She nodded and took a seat. The sight of blood on old bandages made her head feel woozy. Haley looked away and covered her mouth to keep from gagging. She closed her eyes and leaned her head back against the wall.

"Are you okay miss?" a panicked voice asked.

Nodding, her eyes flew open. Her gaze darted around the room. When she spotted the trashcan, she dashed toward it, relieving the contents of her breakfast.

"I'm pretty sure I can guess why you're here without even examining you." The doctor chuckled. "You're free to go soldier."

"Thank you, sir." He hopped off of the doctor's exam table and tipped his hat toward Haley. "Congratulations, ma'am."

Before she could have a coherent thought to respond, he was gone. Who congratulated a person for being ill?

"Would you like for me to help you up on the table?" The doctor patted the table recently vacated.

"No, thank you. I can manage." Haley walked to the table and turned around, carefully scooting herself up on the table. "You said you could already tell what was wrong with me. Do a lot of people get sick from the food or water here?"

Doctor Adams chuckled. "No, but it happens on rare occasion."

"Rare?" Haley asked. "So, I'm one of the few people?"

"Lay down while I examine you?" the doctor said. "When did you begin to feel ill?"

Haley thought about it. "Right around the time we got here."

"How long ago was that?"

"Four weeks," Haley said.

"And have you felt like this every day?"

"Mm…some days."

"Is there anything that makes it worse?" Doctor Adams asked.

"Like the smell of food?" Haley said. "This was the first time I've almost fainted. Something about seeing his blood made me feel all weak inside."

The doctor felt around on her stomach. "Have your breast been tender?"

"My what?" Her cheeks warmed and she quickly sat up. "I beg your pardon."

He smiled, which she didn't find amusing in the least. "I'm sorry." He took a seat in a chair not far from her. "I can't be sure, but I suspect you may be with child?"

"What?" Haley looked down at her belly. She had felt bloated, but pregnant? "I'm not sure I can get pregnant."

"You *have been* with your husband, haven't you?"

She nodded. "We were married two months ago, but my first husband and I had been married for eight years and never conceived."

"Then it appears the problem there was his, not yours." Doctor Adams shrugged. "Because if food were making you sick, you would be better by now. I don't know of any viruses that last this long without causing a person to become dehydrated, and you don't have a problem with frequently releasing your bowels?"

Haley shook her head.

"Then in my opinion, the next obvious explanation is you must be with child."

She blinked several times, not seeing anything but the questions running through her head. How would Malcom feel about this? It would possibly change his plans of taking her on the trail with him. Could she handle him gone for months at a time? It had been unnerving to have him gone for weeks. What if he never came back? The thought of raising their child alone brought tears to her eyes.

Malcom couldn't wait to see Haley when they rode into the fort. The soldiers took Joshua Stanton to the stockade and he went in search of his wife. Four weeks away from Haley was way too long. He was anxious to taste her kisses and feel her body close to his.

"Have you seen my wife?" he asked Lt. Col. Declan McGuire.

"I believe she went to lay down."

"At this time of day?" It was almost supper time.

McGuire shrugged. "I don't believe she has been feeling well lately."

When Malcom found her, she was asleep. He stood over her and stared. The thought of losing her made him tremble. He'd lost one wife, he couldn't handle losing another.

Her eyes fluttered, and she startled upon seeing his figure standing over her.

He sat on the bed beside her and took her hand in his.

"What's wrong, my love?"

"Please, lay by me." Haley scooted over to make room for him and he did as obliged.

"I'm sorry I was gone so long," his voice was strained. How could he make it up to her? "But you'll be happy to know that Joshua Stanton has been taken into custody and the military will make sure he and his men are charged with murder."

She gave a faint smile.

Malcom's throat went dry. What was wrong with his wife? He wanted to know.

"I saw the doctor today," she said.

His body tensed.

"I don't know how to tell you this, other than to come out and say it, but..."

"But what?" He heard the panic in his own voice. He needed to be strong for her. "Whatever it is, we can face it together."

Haley giggled.

Malcom's gaze narrowed like a hawk. She found this amusing?

"The doctor thinks I am with child."

"A baby?"

She nodded.

"But I thought you couldn't have children?"

"It appears I can."

It was his turn to chuckle.

"So, you're happy about this?" Uncertainty shone in her eyes.

"Very." He kissed her. "In fact, if you feel well enough, I'd be happy to recreate what led up to this event.

"We have been apart for a while," she admitted.

"And if I have my way, that will never happen again."

"That's worth it in itself." Haley smiled wide. "Why don't

you show me how much you've missed me?"

Chapter Thirteen

Independence, Missouri — November 1840

*I**ndependence held past memories for*
Haley. When she left the town, she was a widow. Now,
she was married and with child. How different a matter
of months could be in changing someone's life. She thought of
the scripture from Psalms about *joy comes in the morning*. At
one point in her life, it looked hopeless, but now she had been
restored and bursting with new life, both physically and
emotionally.

Galen had remained a man of his word and offered a fatted
calf for a feast. He and Malcom had buried the hatchet. She
prayed regularly for Galen and for God to send him a wife. She
suggested he pray as well and that it took time for God's plans
to work themselves out. But when they did… *He made all
things new.*

She rubbed her rounding belly and smiled.

Malcom's crew gathered around with them and several
others who had gone to Santa Fe to trade. Everyone had
pitched in by bringing a dish to share over their meal of
Thanksgiving. Malcom asked to give a blessing over the meal.

He stood and began praying, "Our Father, which art in

heaven, we thank you for all who are gathered here today with us, and we thank you for keeping us safe upon our journey. I pray that you bless each and every one. I thank you for blessing me with a loving wife and another child, and we especially thank you for justice being served by Your hand and not our..."

Malcom finished with the Lord's Prayer and everyone said, "Amen."

He sat down and took Haley's hand in his. "I know this means a little more travel, but I have been offered a position at the fort to mediate between the military, the Indians and the settlers. It would mean we could have quarters at the fort and would be protected."

"What about the wagon train?" Haley asked.

"I made the mistake of leaving my family before." Malcom's voice grew husky. "I won't make that mistake again."

"Are you sure?"

He nodded. "Four weeks away from you were the longest days of my life. I never want to be apart from you again."

"Nor I, you."

Malcom claimed her lips and her insides melted like butter. Savoring in the sweet delight, she knew would never get tired of him having that effect on her.

The Other Stories in the Thanksgiving Books & Blessings Collection

GONE TO TEXAS
By Caryl McAdoo
GATEWAY TO THE WEST
By Susette Williams
TRAIL TO CLEAR CREEK
By Kit Morgan
HEATH AND HOME
By P. Creeden
NO TURNING BACK
By Lynette Sowell
DAUGHTER OF DEFIANCE
By Heather Blanton
NUGGET NATE: MOYA'S THANKSGIVING PROPOSAL
By George McVey
UNMISTAKABLY YOURS
By Kristin Holt
ESTHER'S TEMPTATION
By Lena Nelson Dooley

*I have a real treat for you, Readers! Here's a sneak Preview of **Kit Morgan's** story in the Thanksgiving Books & Blessings, **Trail to Clear Creek**!*

For your reading pleasure . . .

Chapter One

Independence, Missouri, March 1849

Benedict is dead. My heart bleeds.

But I must go on.

Honoria Alexandra Sayer dipped her pen into the inkwell, eyes on the page before her. She'd written that entry months ago, but her pain at times was still bone-searing deep. She hadn't written in her private diary since.

She put pen to paper and began to write …

Benedict, my love, so much has happened since you left us. The boys insist I decide what to do. Duncan is especially anxious. Our money is nearly gone.

I wish you were here to guide us, but everything is up to me now and Duncan – at least in his mind. He is the oldest and at nineteen, considered a man. He wants to lead, has been doing so, but I can't help feeling that we'll need more. Not that he can't be head of the family, but there's so much missing. So much of you.

Honoria sighed, dipped the pen and continued. She didn't have much time.

Colin and Harrison argue as usual and miss you terribly. Harrison still cries when he thinks no one can see him, and Colin's practical jokes are rampant. He has annoyed Mr. Greenly at the mercantile more than once, and I've had to speak with him about it. I hope their hearts will settle soon.
We must be on our way. I suppose writing to you like this will help me decide what to do. Your dream to come to this country became our dream, my love. And I cannot let that dream die in vain.

"Mother?"

Honoria raised her head. "Yes?"

Her eldest son Duncan stepped into the room. "The others are ready to leave. We made a list of what we'll need. Mr. Greenly said he has a wagon."

She closed her eyes and sighed again. So this was it – Duncan was forcing her hand. "Come here, darling."

He approached, his booted feet heavy against the wooden floor. "Yes, Mother?"

She turned in her chair to look at him. Duncan was tall, taller than his father. "You've grown again."

He put his hand to his chest and shrugged. "Filled out, yes. Taller, no. Not that I've noticed."

She smiled as tears stung the back of her eyes. To her, he was still the little boy that loved animals, saved little damsels in distress (kittens from trees, mostly) and looked out for her as long as she could remember. He was now her knight in shining armor doing his best to fill his father's shoes. "You really want to do this?"

"You do too. You just can't admit it."

Honoria smiled. "You know me so well. But I've made my decision. And you're right – I must have made it days ago and am only now voicing it."

Duncan went down on one knee and took her hands in his. "Mother, we have to do this."

"I know. We haven't a choice."

"There's always a choice, but do you really want to stay here?"

"No." She brushed a lock of his thick dark hair out of his face. He was darkly handsome and turned the heads of women everywhere, both young and old. In England, she and Benedict might have arranged a marriage for him. But she wanted her sons to marry for love, not out of obligation to lands and family.

"Mother?"

"I'm sorry," she said with a shake of her head. "I have so much on my mind."

"You miss him, don't you?"

She swallowed hard. "We all do, darling – you, I think, most of all." She brushed at the lock again.

He stood. "I'm his son. Your heart belonged to him. He but guided mine."

Honoria smiled. "You are a wise man, Duncan. But your father loved each of you boys fiercely, never forget that. It's been more than six months and we have to move on. It's what he would have wanted."

Duncan nodded. "We'll do it, Mother. We'll go west and start a cattle ranch, just as Father planned. We should have left last month."

Honoria got up, crossed the room and opened the top drawer of a dresser. She rummaged through the clothing, pulled out a small bundle and opened it. "This is all the money we have left."

He joined her to stare at their savings. "Will it be enough?"

"I hope so. Supplies can be costly this time of year. Everyone will be scrambling to buy what they can. Have you found out if anyone else is leaving?" She heard the worry in her voice and cleared her throat. But she should be worried – she and her sons had tarried long enough. If there were no other groups leaving Independence at the end of the month, they'd have to stay until next spring. And none of them wanted to do that.

"Yes, there's a Mr. Kinzey whose company is still forming. We'd need to speak with him first, introduce ourselves. Then we have two weeks to prepare."

"That's not much time to get our affairs in order," she said as her eyes gravitated to the diary on her desk. "But we have to do it."

Duncan embraced her. "We'll pull through, Mother. We always do. Besides, this is what we've planned for. It's why we came to this country in the first place."

When he released her, Honoria reached into her dress sleeve for her handkerchief. "Yes, I know." She blew her nose, not bothering to stop her tears. Most had been cried by now anyway. The first few months had been the hardest. Now when they came, they didn't last long.

"Shall I tell Colin and Harrison we're meeting with Mr. Kinzey?"

"Yes, do that. I'll get my shawl."

He touched her shoulder. "Would you like me to carry the money?"

Honoria looked at the bundle in her hand. They'd been following Benedict's plan, living as frugally as they could to make sure they'd have enough for the long journey west. Duncan found a job at Greenly's Mercantile shortly after Benedict died. Between that and some sewing Honoria did for Mrs. Drury, the owner of the boardinghouse, they were able to make ends meet. Benedict's plan had been to head west in March.

When Benedict was killed in a carriage accident last November, she thought those plans would change. For a few months, her heart yearned for her homeland, Sussex in England. But in the end her husband's dream won out.

Honoria handed her son the bundle, wrapped her shawl around her shoulders, and with a bracing breath walked out the door.

Amos Kinzey was a bear of a man with dark eyes, dark hair and whiskers so thick you couldn't see anything below his nose. That a mouth resided under them soon became apparent. "Ya want to do what?" he bellowed. "Ya should have sought me out weeks ago!"

They were in Mr. Kinzey's office, a tiny room he rented over the Independence *Gazette*. Mr. Wainwright, the editor of the newspaper, could be heard barking orders at his assistant below. Hopefully he wasn't barking at Colin or Harrison. They chose to wait downstairs "We're sorry, Mr. Kinzey," Honoria apologized, ignoring the ruckus beneath them. "But we've been undecided about what to do after my husband died."

He nodded sympathetically. "Ah, yer the ones. I remember when it happened. Terrible accident. To get crushed like that…"

Duncan gently put a hand on his mother's shoulder. "Mr. Kinzey, please," he said with a shake of his head.

Honoria smiled at her son in gratitude. "Be that as it may, Mr. Kinzey, we need to join your wagon train. Your company is the last to leave Independence and we cannot linger any longer."

"Why not?" he asked and looked Duncan over. "Ya got three sons, all capable of work. Unless these English boys don't like to get their hands dirty."

"We do what we must," Duncan said sternly. "But living in Independence until next spring isn't what we had in mind, not if we're able to go now."

Mr. Kinzey laughed. "Aye, boy, that's true. And if I say no?"

"Please, Mr. Kinzey," Honoria said. "We won't be any trouble."

"I'm sure ya won't. And I'll admit, I could use a lad like your son, Mrs. Sayer. He's strong and capable-looking. But that isn't the problem."

"Then what is?"

He shrugged. "Yer not married."

"What?" she said in shock. "What does that have to do with anything?"

"Everything, I'm afraid. I run a clean outfit when I take people on. And I've made it a habit to lead only families and single men. *Not* single women. Having them along tends to cause trouble on the road."

Honoria's mouth fell open in shock. "You mean you expect me to get married in order to join your wagon train?"

"Aye, ma'am, I do." He crossed his arms.

Duncan's head jerked back and forth between them. He clearly couldn't believe the man either. Honoria cleared her throat – her voice had a tendency to crack when she spoke while upset. "Mr. Kinzey, I can understand your position, but ..."

"No buts, Mrs. Sayer. The families that hired me to lead their company have their rules and I have mine."

"Rules!" she squeaked, and saw Duncan look worried. She shook her head and tried again. "Rules, you say?"

"Aye, and one of them is: no unwed women. We've got eighteen wagons, Mrs. Sayer, and within those are more than a dozen single men. It's a long journey and ..."

"Just what are you insinuating?" she interjected.

"I ain't *insinuating* anything. I'm telling ya there'll be trouble if ya ain't got a husband to protect ya."

Honoria took a deep breath and let it out slowly to calm herself. "And my sons aren't enough for the job, is that it?"

Mr. Kinzey looked Duncan up and down. "This one, maybe, but I'll need him for guard duty and whatnot. What happens if one or more of the men get it in their head to pay ya a visit one night while yer boy is working?"

Her mouth flopped open again. "Mr. Kinzey!"

"Mrs. Sayer, I'm not implying ya'd be willing. I *am* implying that after a long time on the road, some men won't care if yer willing or not."

"I ... you ..." Honoria snapped her mouth shut and sighed. "I see your point."

"I'm sorry I can't help ya, ma'am. Yer a nice family, folks around here all say so."

"Say no more, Mr. Kinzey," Honoria said. "I understand." She turned and began to march away.

Mr. Kinzey studied her retreating form. "What's she doing?"

Duncan sighed. "You made her angry."

"Is that bad?"

Duncan shrugged. "It all depends on *how* angry."

A door slammed, followed by the sound of stomping down wooden stairs. Mr. Kinzey scratched his beard. "How angry is that?"

Duncan glanced at the door to the stairs. "I dare say she's, as you Americans put it, 'mad as a rattler' right now. The last time she was this upset, we wound up sailing for America."

"What?" he said in surprise. "But weren't ya planning on doing that anyway?"

"No, it was only my father's dream to come here, go west and start a cattle ranch. It was my mother that made it happen."

"How so?" Mr. Kinzey asked.

Duncan smiled. "Because first she had to make my father believe it *could* happen. And it did." He turned on his heel and headed for the door.

Honoria paced her room. "Get married? I've never heard of anything so ridiculous!" She sat on the bed, put her face in her hands and blew through her fingers. "That wretched man! What do I do now?" She got up, paced some more, then stopped in the middle of the room. "But what if … NO! No, I can't!"

"Can't what, Mother?"

She turned to find Harrison, her youngest, standing in the doorway. She often left it open when one or more of her sons were in the boardinghouse. "What is it, darling?"

"Colin is in trouble with Mr. Greenly again," he said calmly. "I tried to tell him not to toss the ball to me so close to the windows, but …"

"Windows!" Honoria shut her eyes with a grimace. This would be the fourth time in several months Colin had broken a window. She was surprised Mr. Greenly hadn't fired Duncan. But then, Duncan wasn't the one breaking glass; Colin was.

"That lad will be the death of me," she muttered and reached for her shawl.

"No, don't say that," Harrison said, eyes wide as he stepped into the room. "Never."

Honoria studied her son's look of panic. "Oh, Harrison darling, I didn't mean to make it sound as if something would happen to me."

He looked at the floor. "I know – it's just that …"

She went over, put a finger under his chin and lifted his face, though at twelve he was as tall as she. Colin was taller still, and Duncan was towering. "You poor darling, I know what you meant. And I'm not going anywhere." She pulled him into her arms and gave him a hug.

Each of her sons was different. Duncan was a born leader, quiet, strong, discerning and decisive. Harrison was more emotional, passionate about the things he loved and easily riled. And Colin, easier-going than his brothers, was always into some sort of mischief. You never knew what he was thinking until he opened his mouth. He was inventive, could come up with all sorts of ideas when something needed fixing or a problem had to be solved – or when he felt like creating one.

"Things are going to be different now, Harrison," she said into his hair. "We'll get added to Mr. Kinzey's company, you'll see."

"But Mother, Duncan said Mr. Kinzey wanted you to get married. You're not going to, are you?"

She swallowed hard. "We'll try everything we can to make it work, darling. That means … well, that I'll do what I have to, to see we get to where your father wanted us."

He arched an eyebrow. "Does that mean no?"

She smiled. "It means I'm doing my best to make this journey happen."

Harrison cautiously nodded. "Right, then – whatever it takes, Mother. I know none of us would want to disappoint Father."

"No, none of you would ever want to do that." She put a hand on his shoulder and kissed his cheek. "Now we'd best get your brother out of whatever trouble he's gotten himself into."

Harrison smiled. "Yes, I suppose we should." He made a face. "Do we have to?"

She rolled her eyes. "Yes, my love, we do. You and Colin might not see eye to eye, but he's still your brother. Now let's go." She took her shawl from its peg, wrapped it around her shoulders and ushered her son out the door.

When they reached the mercantile, Mr. Greenly, a heavy-set man with salt-and-pepper hair, had Colin sitting on a pickle barrel near the front counter, peeling potatoes. "So does the punishment fit the crime?" she asked.

Mr. Greenly pointed toward the back of the building. "Down the hall, through the storeroom and to the right, Mrs. Sayer."

Honoria eyed her middle son, who grinned sheepishly, dropped some potato peelings into one bowl on the counter and put the finished potato into another. She took a deep breath, headed for the storeroom and groaned. "Oh no, not again!"

Harrison rushed in behind her, eyes wide, and saw the mess on the floor. "Blimey, he really did it this time!"

"Harrison, watch your tongue," she scolded as she studied the damage. Colin had indeed broken the glass in the window. Again. The boy was a disaster. "Oh dear …"

Mr. Greenly leaned against the doorjamb behind them. "You realize I'll have to tack something over that window again, Mrs. Sayer."

She looked at him with a heavy sigh. "Yes, I know. And once again, I apologize. I just don't know what's gotten into that …" Oh, but she did know what had gotten into Colin – this was his way of dealing with grief. Duncan kept his bottled up,

Harrison wore his on his sleeve. And Colin acted out. "Well, if it's any consolation, Mr. Greenly, we'll be leaving soon. You'll not suffer broken windows at the hand of my son after that."

"Leaving? But I thought you didn't, er, meet Amos Kinzey's qualifications," he said.

She stared at him a moment. "And how, may I ask, do you know that?"

He shrugged. "I run the mercantile, Mrs. Sayer. I hear everything."

"Not from my sons, I hope."

"No, from Amos Kinzey."

"Oh." She rolled her eyes. "Why am I not surprised?"

He shrugged again. "Regardless, you'll still have to replace the window."

She tapped her foot a few times. "I don't suppose he can work it off?" After all, they'd need all their money to buy supplies for the long journey. A little extra wouldn't hurt.

"I already got him peeling them 'taters for the missus – she's upstairs making supper. In fact, I'd best fetch them to her. Excuse me."

"Yes, of course," she said with another look at the window. She'd been so wrapped up worrying about the needed supplies, she hadn't given much thought to what their arrival in Oregon Territory would entail. They'd need quite a lot of things, now that she thought of it, and had only discussed a few with Benedict before he died. He was planning to make a final list that very week so they could budget their money – money that was now quickly dwindling. Paying for a broken window (again!) just added to it.

With a heavy sigh, Honoria took Harrison by the hand and marched back to the storefront. No time to lose.

Another historical romance series …

Mail Order Brides:
Jessie's Bride
Excerpt:

CHAPTER ONE

House Springs, Missouri —1843

Jessie Kincaid stared at the captivating picture of Sarah Engle, his future wife. While the drawing was done with pencil, she'd told him her eyes were blue and her hair was blonde. He envisioned gently tugging on one of the curling tendrils piled up on her head and it bouncing back into place. He smiled, laid her picture aside and began to write.

My Dearest Sarah,

Your picture along with your letters, and getting to know you, has only served to capture my heart. I know we can build a wonderful life together. I have enclosed a ticket for the stagecoach, along with ten dollars so that you can have some money for your journey. I look forward to seeing you. I am anxious to start our new life together and cannot wait to finally see you face to face.

All my love,

Jessie

He folded the letter and placed it, along with the stagecoach ticket, inside the envelope.

Being the youngest of four had its drawbacks, especially since he didn't have any sisters for his brothers to fuss over. It meant his brothers' overbearing, protective side was focused on him, whether or not he wanted to deal with their interference in his life.

Jessie never knew the one sister their parents had the year before he was born. She'd caught pneumonia and died before Ma became with child with him. If she had lived, his brothers would have focused on her and not Jessie. But since they didn't have a sister, they focused on him, the baby of the family.

Out west, there were twice as many men folk as women. Perhaps even a few less in their town. Long hours tending cattle didn't give much chance to cultivate a proper relationship with a woman, much less with competition for the few handsome women there were in town.

None of his brothers were married, even though his oldest brother was twenty-eight, a mere four years older. How would they handle him getting hitched before they did? Moreover, how would Ma handle it, especially since she hadn't even met her future daughter-in-law? He would have told them he was writing a mail order bride except he didn't want to endure the ribbing his brothers would have given him.

Sarah would be there in a couple of weeks. That didn't give him long to break the news and let it simmer in before they had a chance to meet her. Hopefully by then, his brothers would be on their best behavior. He could hope.

Jessie folded the envelope and stuffed it in his pocket before heading to the kitchen for vittles.

"Smells good, Ma." He gave her a brief sideways hug and brushed a kiss upon her cheek, then snitched a piece of bacon off the plate.

"Don't think I didn't see that, youngin'." Ma smiled and brushed a few stray hairs away from her face with the back of her hand. She always wore her hair in a bun, ready for work.

Jessie winked at Ma and took a bite. "The whole point of cookin' is to eat it."

"Well, let her finish cookin' so we all can eat." Marshall sounded gruff, but Jessie knew his brother had a tendency to show his dominance. Which was needed to help keep the peace in his job as sheriff. Being the oldest Kincaid boy, keeping his three younger brothers in line, had prepared him for the role.

Out of all his kin, Jessie feared telling Marshall about his fiancée more than anyone else. Marshall figured most people had an angle, and he'd want to check Sarah out before he'd give his approval.

Jessie turned twenty-four last month, he wasn't getting any younger. Pa was only forty-two when he died eleven years ago. If Jessie wanted a family, and wanted to have time to enjoy them, he needed to get started. Maybe it was better to wait and tell his family until Sarah was here, then they couldn't do anything. Marshall would understand the law, and the legal ramifications of breaking an engagement. Not that Sarah would take him to court for a broken love pledge, but her pa might. Marshall would have to allow Jessie to go through with the marriage.

"What are you grinning about?" Caleb asked as he

and Montana came in from the outside and both took a seat at the table.

Jessie hadn't realized he was smiling. If he wasn't careful, he'd end up giving himself away.

Marshall got up and grabbed the plate of biscuits and bacon from Ma and set them on the table. "He's grinning 'cause he got away with snitching vittles before everyone else." Marshall playfully slapped the back of Jessie's head. "Take your hat off and say grace."

Jessie obliged, placing his hat on the back post of his chair. He smiled as he said the prayer over their meal, silently adding a special thanks for his bride-to-be.

All of Susette's Books

The 12 Mysteries of Christmas ~
IN THE NICK OF TIME – Book 1
STARR WITNESS – Book 7

Novellas ~
ACCIDENTAL MEETING
SCROOGE FALLS IN LOVE – Typecast Christmas
series
SHADOWS OF DOUBT
MORE THAN FRIENDS
LITTLE ORPHAN ANNIE
A STITCH IN TIME
GATEWAY TO THE WEST – Thanksgiving Books &
Blessings series

Novels~
SOMETHING ABOUT SAM
HONORABLE INTENTIONS

Reach out to the author!

Website
http://www.susettewilliams.com/

Facebook
https://www.facebook.com/AuthorSusetteWilliams/
(You can subscribe to my newsletter through my
Facebook page or my author page.)

Twitter
https://twitter.com/SusetteWilliams

Author Pages: *(please follow)*

Amazon
https://www.amazon.com/SusetteWilliams/e/B008RS
AZW0/

BookBub
https://www.bookbub.com/profile/susette-williams

Email
contactme@susettewilliams.com

Author reaching out to you!

Dear Readers!

I hope you have enjoyed reading GATEWAY TO THE WEST as much as I have enjoyed writing it. I love stories of second chances. Haley and Malcom both understood loneliness and loss. God brought them together, meeting both of their needs, and giving them someone else who understood their grief.

Before we were married, my husband was praying for a wife because he was lonely. I was dating someone who was not leading a godly life and prayed to have the strength to walk away from the relationship. God answered both of our prayers and brought us together. I am thankful for my husband and for thirty-five wonderful years together. The years have been wonderful because he has been by my side, even through the many trials and storms of life that we have faced. God may not always answer our prayers the way we think He should, but He knows our needs and has a plan for our lives.

May you be blessed and your heart content.

Blessings,
Susette

Printed in Great Britain
by Amazon

46791545R00057